Long ago, in a distant land, lived a young King and his daughter, Ivy. The King's beloved wife had died when Ivy was just a few years old. Ivy missed her mother dearly and the King was concerned about his daughter's happiness. He thought to himself, "I don't want my daughter to be lonely, so the castle will be open to all the village children. They will always be welcome here."

Before long the castle was filled with children.
Many of them had never seen such splendor.
For them, the castle was truly a magical place
and their excited, playful voices could be heard everywhere.
"Wow, I've never seen anything like this before!"
"It's incredible!" "Hey, Ivy, this is a great place. Can I fish in the pond?"
2 "Of course you can, Joey!"

Being good-natured, kind and honest, Ivy made friends easily. She always had company at mealtimes, and slumber parties were frequent happenings. The children busily explored the castle's many rooms, playing endless games of hide-and-seek.

"You're 'it' this time, Joey."
"Okay, Ivy, but you'd better find a good place to hide."

The fun-filled years passed quickly and on Ivy's thirteenth birthday, her father gave a party in her honor. Her friends dressed up in their very best clothes and each arrived with a lovely present. There were clowns, animals, wonderful magicians, and lots of ice cream and cake.

Before the night was over, the King took his daughter aside. "Ivy, I have a very special present for you. It's the golden wedding band that belonged to your mother."

Overcome with joy, she gasped, "It's so beautiful! I'll never, ever, take it off!" Her friends gathered round to admire the gift.

A few days later, Ivy and her best friend Lisa, were playing ball in the garden. As Ivy reached out to catch the ball, the ring slipped off her finger. It sailed through the air and landed in the pond with a sad little plop.

Watching it sink before her eyes, Ivy cried out in horror—"Oh no! This is terrible! I lost my mother's ring! What will I tell my father?"

Lisa wanted desperately to help Ivy find the ring. Reaching into the water as far as her little arm could stretch, she said with a sigh, "I'm sorry Ivy, but this pond's too dark and too deep. I can't see or feel a thing. It's hopeless."

"Excuse me. *Ribbit. Ribbit.* Perhaps I can help."
The startled children looked at each other, wondering who spoke. Then, at the edge of the pond, something moved. "Look! It's a Frog!" shouted Lisa, pointing to it. And so it was; a talking Frog at that!

The Frog looked at Ivy, longingly. "I'll help you find the ring if you'll do something for me. It's very lonely out here in the pond. I have no friends of my own. Will you come to visit me? *Ribbit. Ribbit,*" he ribbited.

"Of course I will!"
"Promise?"
"Cross my heart and hope to die!"

So without hesitation the Frog dove to the bottom of the pond and, within seconds, up he came clutching the cherished ring.

"Oh, you've found it! Thank you so much. I'll never forget you for this!" Ivy and Lisa were so relieved they ran back to the castle laughing.

That night at dinner, Ivy told her father and friends about the adventure with the talking Frog. When she finished, Joey said, "That's the strangest story I've ever heard!" And Denise remarked, "Are you sure it was a real Frog?"

"We're sure," replied Lisa and Ivy at the exact same time.

Hugging his daughter the King said, "Ivy, I would have been very sad if you'd lost your mother's ring, but I'm glad everything turned out well."

"I'll be more careful next time, Daddy. I promise."

The dinner had ended and the children readied themselves for bed. School was starting in the morning and they were looking forward to the first day.

For several months, Ivy and her friends were busy learning many new things. With little time to play, the promise to the Frog had been forgotten. Fall turned to winter, and winter to spring. Before long, it was summer.

One day, as Lisa was walking by the pond, she came upon the Frog. "You look awful. Are you sick?"

The sad-looking Frog replied, "The Princess has forgotten her promise to me. Now I'm more lonely than ever. *Ribbit*."

Feeling terrible Lisa left the Frog and ran off to find her friend. Ivy was in her room playing. As soon as Lisa saw her, she told her about the poor Frog. "The Frog helped you and you promised to visit him. You didn't keep your word. Now his feelings are hurt."

Ivy was crushed. She had never broken a promise to anyone before. That night, as she was laying in her bed, Ivy thought of the Frog. "I've been very selfish. I have lots of friends to play with, and a father who loves me. The poor Frog has no one. I've got to make it up to him."

With that last thought, she fell into a restless sleep.

The next morning, Ivy woke early. She dressed quickly and ran down to the pond to find the Frog. Though she searched frantically, he was nowhere to be found. In desperation she said, "I've looked everywhere and still can't find him. I'll have to get my friends to help."

Lisa and the other children soon joined the search. They were so concerned for the poor Frog that they didn't notice the time pass.

"Where can he be," Denise wondered. Completely baffled, Joey shook his head and replied, "I give up! We've gone over every inch of this garden !"

Just as it was getting dark, they heard a lonely, croaking sound, *"Ribbit, ribbit, ribbit."*

"Look. It's him," shouted Ivy. In her excitement, she reached out for the Frog, grabbed him, and gave him a great big kiss!

Suddenly, in a flash of light and a cloud of smoke, where once stood the Frog, now stood a handsome young Prince! It was truly a magical moment!

Turning toward Ivy, the Prince explained, "I've been living in this pond for years. An evil sorcerer put a curse on me, but you have freed me with your kiss! Thank you, Ivy. Thank you, everyone!"

That night at dinner, the new guest was seated next to Ivy.
She turned to the Prince and said, "I have learned a valuable lesson
from you. Friends are very important people, and a promise made,
should be a promise kept."

All around the table, voices were raised in agreement:
"Let's hear it for Ivy!"
"She's a real, true friend!"
"We'll be friends forever!"

The King sat back, smiling to himself, and thought, "Looks like I got my wish. My daughter will never be lonely again!"
And so it would be!

The End